VIVIAN WALSH

JUNE AND AUGUST

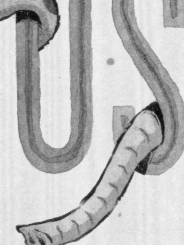

ILLUSTRATED BY ADAM McCAULEY

Abrams Books for Young Readers, New York

The illustrations in this book were made with
scratchboard, colored pencil, and gouache on paper.

Library of Congress Cataloging-in-Publication Data

Walsh, Vivian.
June and August / by Vivian Walsh ; illustrated by Adam McCauley.
p. cm.
Summary: Two animals who share a love of the night sky meet in the daylight
and are surprised to discover how different they are.
ISBN 978-0-8109-8410-3
[1. Friendship—Fiction. 2. Individuality—Fiction. 3. Elephants—Fiction.
4. Snakes—Fiction.] I. McCauley, Adam, ill. II. Title.

PZ7.W168945Jun 2009
[E]—dc22
2008044287

Book design by Chad W. Beckerman

Printed and bound in China
10 9 8 7 6 5 4 3 2 1

Abrams Books for Young Readers are available at special discounts when purchased in quantity for
premiums and promotions as well as fundraising or educational use. Special editions can also be
created to specification. For details, contact specialmarkets@hnabooks.com or the address below.

harry n. abrams, inc.
a subsidiary of La Martinière Groupe

115 West 18th Street
New York, NY 10011
www.hnabooks.com

To daisies underfoot,
to stars overhead,
and Zoe in between.

Special note to Zoe,

and everyone else who is not Zoe:

Love the creatures big and small,

that's the long and short of it.

— V.W.

For Wig

— A.M.

June and August met one evening.
It was dark and the stars were bright.

June was thrilled to see a shooting star.

August loved the moon.
"It's so big and round."

"If I was in space," said June,
"I'd go as fast as a shooting star,
leaving a tail of light behind me."

"Well, if I was in space," said August,
"I'd run round the moon."

The two new friends agreed
to meet the very next day.

It was too dark to see what August
looked like, so June asked, "How will
I know you in the daylight?"

"I am very handsome," said August.

"And I," said June, "am very clever."

The next day, August looked for his new friend.
He saw many clever-looking creatures.

Which one was June?

June looked for August.
She didn't see any animals that looked
handsome, or at least, none as
good-looking as she.

August waited for June.
August didn't mind waiting.
It was a beautiful day.

June did not like to wait.

Where was August?

"It's such a gray day," bellyached the snake.
"What is this strange cloud hanging over
my head?"

The cloud rumbled,
and from it came a voice,
and it said, "JUNE?"

"GIANT?" asked June.

"No, I'm not giant. I'm just August.
And what are you?
Are you all trunk, or all tail?"

"I am all me!" said June.

"We are very different," said August.

June looked at their shadows.
She noticed they both started and ended the same way.
"It's mostly in the middle that we're different," said June.

"And the feet," said August, lifting each one
to show June what he was talking about.

"Yesssss," hissed June, as she silently counted
the large and impressive stumps.
"One, two, three, four . . . da feet."

August suggested a walk.

June suggested slithering toward the jungle.

June loved tying knots.

"Look at me," said August. "I'm entwined in vines."

June thought August looked stunning.

"The others are looking at us," said June.

"Yes, we must look GRAND," said August.

"Let's run to the top of the hill!" said August,
who was itching to use his big elephant feet.

"I can't get up there," said June.
"It's too far and too high."

"Not if your new friend is an elephant.
Climb on my back."

"Why do you climb the mountain?" asked June.

"You'll see," answered August.

The moon rose.

A star blazed across the sky.

"Are we in space now?" asked June.

"Nearer," said August.

It was dark and the stars were bright.
The two friends liked what they could see.

June and August agreed to meet the very next day.